Dear Parents:

P9-DHN-614

Congratulations! Your child is taking the first steps on an exciting journey. The destination? Independent reading!

STEP INTO READING® will help your child get there. The program offers five steps to reading success. Each step includes fun stories and colorful art or photographs. In addition to original fiction and books with favorite characters, there are Step into Reading Non-Fiction Readers, Phonics Readers and Boxed Sets, Sticker Readers, and Comic Readers—a complete literacy program with something to interest every child.

Learning to Read, Step by Step!

Ready to Read   Preschool–Kindergarten
• big type and easy words • rhyme and rhythm • picture clues
For children who know the alphabet and are eager to begin reading.

Reading with Help   Preschool–Grade 1
• basic vocabulary • short sentences • simple stories
For children who recognize familiar words and sound out new words with help.

Reading on Your Own   Grades 1–3
• engaging characters • easy-to-follow plots • popular topics
For children who are ready to read on their own.

Reading Paragraphs   Grades 2–3
• challenging vocabulary • short paragraphs • exciting stories
For newly independent readers who read simple sentences with confidence.

Ready for Chapters   Grades 2–4
• chapters • longer paragraphs • full-color art
For children who want to take the plunge into chapter books but still like colorful pictures.

STEP INTO READING® is designed to give every child a successful reading experience. The grade levels are only guides; children will progress through the steps at their own speed, developing confidence in their reading.

Remember, a lifetime love of reading starts with a single step!

© 2019 Universal City Studios LLC. All Rights Reserved.

Published in the United States by Random House Children's Books, a division of Penguin Random House LLC, 1745 Broadway, New York, NY 10019, and in Canada by Penguin Random House Canada Limited, Toronto.

Step into Reading, Random House, and the Random House colophon are registered trademarks of Penguin Random House LLC.

Visit us on the Web!
StepIntoReading.com
rhcbooks.com

Educators and librarians, for a variety of teaching tools, visit us at RHTeachersLibrarians.com

ISBN 978-1-9848-9511-0 (trade) — ISBN 978-1-9848-9512-7 (lib. bdg.) — ISBN 978-1-9848-9513-4 (ebook)

Printed in the United States of America
10 9 8 7 6 5 4 3 2 1

Random House Children's Books supports the First Amendment and celebrates the right to read.

STEP INTO READING®

Step 2 · READING WITH HELP

ILLUMINATION PRESENTS
THE SECRET LIFE OF
PETS 2

QUEEN of CATS!

by Dennis R. Shealy

Random House New York

Gidget was a small
white dog.
She lived in
an apartment
in New York City.

Lots of pets lived
in the building . . .

. . . but Max the dog
was Gidget's best friend.

Max had lots of toys.
Busy Bee was his
favorite.

One day, Max's brother, Duke, told him they were going on a trip.

Max dug through his toys.
He wanted Gidget
to watch Busy Bee for him.

Gidget had a great time
playing with Busy Bee
until . . . the toy fell
out the window!

Busy Bee fell into an apartment that was filled with cats.

Gidget was afraid to go in.
Cats roamed the place
day and night.

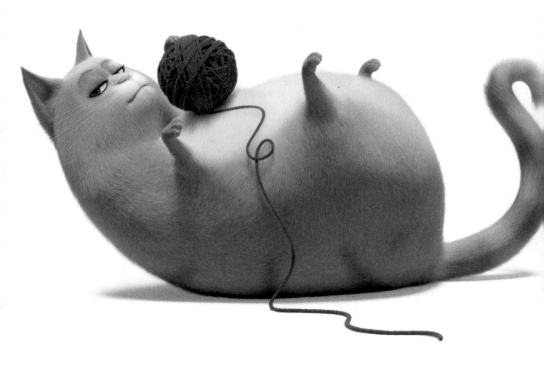

Gidget needed help.

She went to her friend

Chloe the cat.

She had to get
Busy Bee back.
Chloe could teach her
how to be a cat.

Sweetpea, Buddy,
and Mel agreed to help
Chloe teach Gidget.

Mel thought eating chips
was a good place to start.
Oh, Mel.

Chloe said Gidget

had to look like a cat.

She put on pink cat ears,
and a white sock for a tail.

Chloe taught Gidget

how to bother

humans . . .

. . . and use a litter box.

Oh, Mel!

Gidget was ready
to get Busy Bee back!
And she had a secret
weapon . . .

. . . the laser pointer.

When Norman lit it up,

Gidget ate the red dot.

The cats were amazed!

They brought
Busy Bee to her
and named Gidget
Queen of Cats!

© UCS LLC

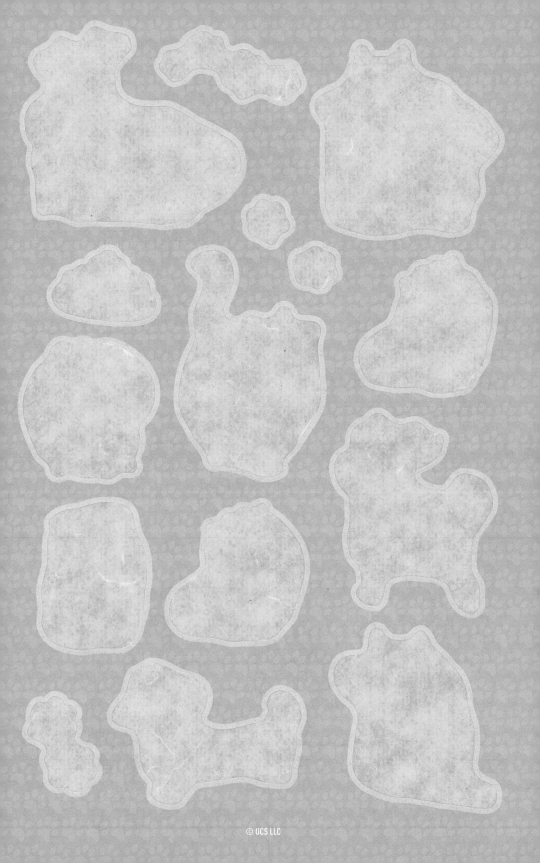

© UCS LLC

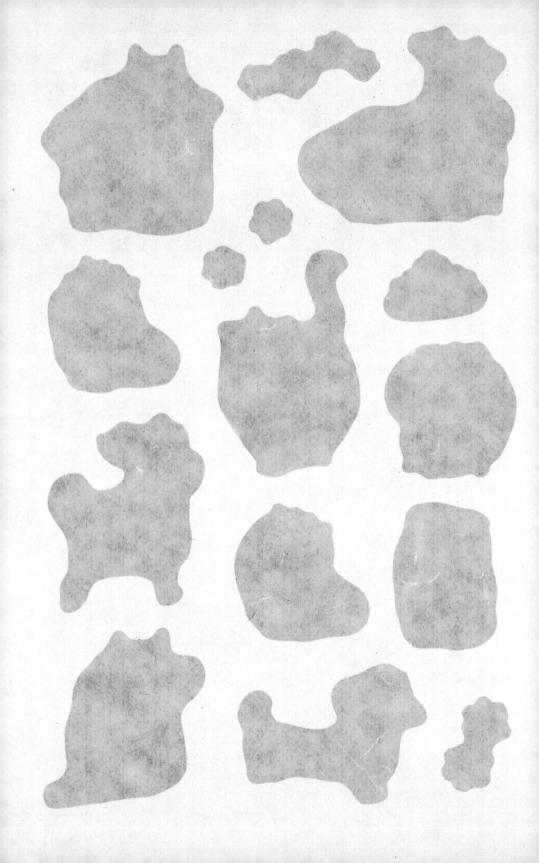